Scary Stories to Tell if Y

Sequel to Scary Stories to Tell if You Dare

Collected from folklore and retold by Joe Oliveto
Illustration designs by Joe Oliveto
Copyright © 2017 by Joe Oliveto

TABLE OF CONTENTS

ANOTHER CAMPFIRE

When I wrote the first *Scary Stories to Tell if You Dare*, my goal was to offer readers the kind of experience that books like *Scary Stories to Tell in the Dark* and other classics of children's folklore offered me as a child. I hoped readers would enjoy another collection of creepy urban legends and ghost stories as much as I enjoyed researching and writing it.

The response was overwhelmingly positive. People throughout the world say the book perfectly evoked the classics of their childhood.

I've loved scary stories for as long as I can possibly remember. I'll be reading them and sharing them for the rest of my life. Thanks to the internet, it's easier than ever to find terrifying legends from all corners of the globe. Reading and telling these stories doesn't just allow us to enjoy a good scare. These stories offer a glimpse into other cultures.

Books like *Scary Stories to Tell in the Dark* appealed to my love of creepy tales, while igniting my love of folklore. I hope this book does the same for you.

Joe Oliveto
New York, NY
December 4, 2017

THE EDGE OF THIS WORLD

Although these stories can't be true, some claim they are...

Every year, Barry and Conklin would go up to the mountains for a few days to hunt deer. One day Conklin returned from the mountains without Barry. He told everyone Barry had gone missing. The police put together a search party, but the heavy winter snow came just as they started to look for Barry. They didn't find any trace of him for months.

The police finally found his body in the spring. He was lying against a tree deep in the woods. Someone had broken his skull. He still had his rifle, but his favorite hunting knife was gone. Everyone thought Conklin must have killed him, but they could never prove it.

Conklin went back up to the mountains later that year. This time, he brought his friend Ed. They spent the first day hiking deep into the woods to set up camp. Ed got so tired that he went to sleep early.

A few hours later he woke up to the sound of Conklin screaming, "Don't do it! Please don't do it!"

It was too dark to see anything. Ed found his flashlight and got out of his tent. He found Conklin lying against a nearby tree. He was dead. A hunting knife had been pushed deep into his heart.

Ed brought the police to Conklin's body. When they dusted the knife for fingerprints, they were shocked by what they found.

The fingerprints belonged to Barry.

THE BULLET

Henry and Emily had been married for years. One day Henry decided to leave her. He met someone else and wanted to marry her instead. Emily begged him not to leave, but Henry didn't listen.

Emily was so heartbroken that she killed herself. Her brother swore to his family he would get his revenge on Henry.

Emily's brother went to Henry's home later that year. He planned to kill him.

When he arrived at Henry's house, he found him working out in the yard. Emily's brother fired his gun at Henry. The first shot missed. The bullet hit a tree and got stuck there. Emily's brother tried again, but Henry managed to run off. He told the police what happened, and Emily's brother went to jail.

Years later, Henry decided he wanted more space in his yard. He got out his saw to cut down some trees. One tree was so big that a saw wasn't going to be strong enough to bring it down. Henry used dynamite instead.

As soon as he set off the explosion, he felt something hit him right in the chest. He looked down and saw blood pouring onto his shirt. In a few moments, he was dead.

The bullet from years earlier had been stuck in the tree. The explosion caused it to shoot right back into Henry.

CAMPING

When I was in college my friends and I liked to go camping. We would try to find spots that were supposed to be haunted. We thought it was fun to tell ghost stories around the fire until someone got too scared.

There was one forest nearby we always wanted to camp in. It was close to an old road that not many people used anymore. People said there were plenty of ghosts in that area. We didn't really believe them, but we thought it would be fun to camp there anyway.

One weekend we all got together and headed to the woods with our camping gear. That night we made a fire and told stories like we always did. It was getting pretty late, and we were almost ready to go to sleep, when someone walked out of the woods and found our campsite.

At first we were scared, but we quickly realized this person was some sort of police officer or forest ranger. He was dressed in that kind of clothing.

"Doing some camping?" he asked.

We told him we were. We thought it was allowed out there.

The man said it was, but that we should also be careful. He said a lot of bad people hung out in those woods too.

He left us alone after that. Soon, we all went to sleep.

The next morning we headed back to the college. We stopped at a restaurant for breakfast on the way.

The folks at the restaurant asked if we'd been out ghost hunting. They said a lot of the college students did that kind of thing.

We told them we were. When they asked if we had seen anything, we said we hadn't, but we did tell them about the man who visited us at our campsite.

They thought that was strange. Not many officers patrolled those woods anymore. When they asked what the man's clothing looked like, I noticed a picture on the wall. The man in it looked exactly like the man who visited our campsite.

When I told them this, they just looked back at us in shock.

"That's not possible," the man who owned the restaurant said. The man in that picture was part of the forest patrol, but there was no forest patrol like that anymore. He said the picture was more than fifty years old.

BLACK EYES

Megan had just gone to bed. She was almost asleep when she heard a knock at the door.

"I wonder who could be at the door so late," she said. Megan never got visitors at that hour.

She headed to the door and opened it up. Standing on her front porch were two children. One was a girl, who looked to be about six years old. The other was a boy. He looked a couple years older.

For some reason, Megan was scared of them right away. She wasn't sure why. They were just kids, after all. But somehow, it seemed like they wanted to hurt her.

"We need to come in," the boy said. His voice was very polite. Megan thought he almost sounded more like an adult than a child.

"Why do you need to come in?" Megan asked.

"Our mother will be worried about us. We need to use your phone and call her."

"Why are you out so late?" Megan still wasn't sure why these children scared her so much. She felt like she was looking at someone truly evil. Usually, she would be happy to let two children call their mother. But something about these children was different.

"Just let us in. Our mother is worried," the boy said. The girl didn't seem like she was going to talk at all. She just looked like she was watching the boy.

"I don't let strangers into my house," Megan said. "Tell me your mother's number. I'll call her for you."

"No," the boy said. He sounded angry now. "Let us in."

Suddenly, Megan realized why she was so afraid of these children. She couldn't understand why she didn't notice it before.

Their eyes were completely black. There was no color at all.

Megan felt a chill. It was like they had her in a trance before. She knew it should not have taken her that long to notice their eyes.

"You can't come in," Megan said. She was sure they would try to hurt her if she let them in. She didn't know why they didn't just force their way into the house.

"Let us in now," the boy said.

"No!" Megan quickly shut the door.

As soon as she had, the boy started pounding on it. "Let us in!" he shouted. "Let us in!"

Megan wanted to run to the phone, but she was too scared to move. She thought if she turned her back, the boy might open the door and attack her.

He pounded on the door for a long time. It might have just been minutes, but it felt like hours. Then, suddenly, he stopped.

After a moment, Megan stepped to the window next to the door and looked out. There was no sign of them.

ANNIE'S HOUSE

Every child in the neighborhood knew the stories about the deserted house. People said a woman named Annie used to live there. She had five children who she loved very much. One day there was a big fire. Annie got out, but her children didn't.

She went insane after they died. The stories said her ghost still wandered the alleys in the neighborhood at night, looking for her children.

Again, every kid around knew the stories, and knew to avoid the house. Every kid except Danny.

He had just moved to the neighborhood with his family. No one had told him about the house yet.

One night, a few days after moving in, Danny told his parents he was going to go for a walk around the neighborhood. He hadn't seen much of it yet.

"Okay," his mother said," but be back soon."

"I will," Danny said.

It was a dark night. The neighborhood was quiet. Danny thought he might find some other kids playing, but no one was out.

Most of the houses were just like his. Except for one house at the end of the street. It looked empty. There were no lights on. The grass on the lawn hadn't been cut in a long time. And it looked like there must have been a fire in part of the house at some point.

Danny loved to explore these types of places. His parents told him not to, but sometimes he did anyway.

There was a fence around the house, but Danny was able to climb over it easily.

Something about the place scared him already. But he was too curious not to take a closer look. Danny walked up to the porch and tried the door. It opened easily.

The inside of the house was dark. Too dark. For a moment, Danny almost turned back.

Then he heard a voice. "Where are my children?" it asked. It sounded like it was coming from upstairs.

"I'm sorry?" Danny said.

"Where are my children?"

"Is someone here?" Danny wanted to walk away, but he couldn't.

"Do you know where my children are?" The voice sounded like it was getting closer.

A door opened at the top of the stairs. It was too dark to see clearly, but it looked like a woman stepped out. She started walking slowly down the stairs. Danny just stood watching her.

"Where are my children? Have you seen them?" she asked.

"I'm sorry, I have to go," Danny said.

The woman kept getting closer and closer. Danny still couldn't see her clearly.

"Are you one of my children?" she asked.

"No," Danny said. Even though he wanted to run away, he couldn't stop watching her. He was afraid to turn his back on her.

She reached the bottom of the steps. She took a step towards Danny.

Now he could see her face clearly. It was a terrible sight. Her eyes were sunken in. Her black hair looked like the tall, messy grass on her lawn. Most of her teeth were missing. The teeth she did have were rotten.

Finally, Danny was able to move. He let out a scream and dashed towards the fence.

"Are you my child?" the voice called out behind him.

Danny almost reached the fence when he tripped over a fallen branch. He tried to pull himself back up, but before he could, a cold hand grabbed him from behind and started dragging him towards the house.

He tried to get away, but the hand held him tight.

As Annie dragged him back to her house, she kept repeating the same words: "Where are my children? Where are my children?"

She brought Danny back into the house and closed the door behind her. No one ever saw Danny again.

HIDDEN

Hunters were going missing in the woods around the village. Sometimes people found fresh human bones out there. But most of the time they didn't find anything at all.

After a while, most hunters refused to go out to the woods. They said there was a monster out there that snatched up people and brought them back to its lair to be eaten.

One man wasn't afraid. He didn't believe stories like that. He said it was probably just a big animal attacking people. He told everyone in the village that he would go out and kill it if they promised a big reward.

The villagers were desperate. If people couldn't hunt, they couldn't eat. They told him they would pay him a big fortune if he killed the monster.

The hunter accepted their offer. He headed out to the woods one night and set up camp. It was late, and he decided he would sleep first. The next morning, he would find the animal that had been killing so many other hunters.

He didn't sleep well. There were strange noises all throughout the night. Sometimes he even thought he heard human screams.

"Don't be foolish," he told himself. "All those stories are just made up."

The next morning he went out in search of the animal. He walked for miles through the forest, looking for signs of it. He was getting far away from camp by this point.

Most people would have been scared to go out there alone. There didn't need to be monsters for them to be scared. A person could easily get lost in the woods if they weren't careful.

But the hunter knew the forest well. He wasn't worried about that.

Still, he was starting to get a bad feeling. It seemed to him like he kept seeing some sort of animal or person out of the corner of his eye. The problem was, when he turned to look at it, it was nowhere in sight.

"Your mind is just playing tricks on you," he told himself. "You just listened to too many stories."

But he kept seeing the thing, whatever it was. It seemed like it was getting closer. It would always appear for a moment, right in the corner of his eye, where he couldn't get a good look. He couldn't even tell if it looked like a person or an animal. But it was always gone whenever he tried to spot it.

Then he started hearing its footsteps.

Before, it had been too far away to hear anything. Now, whenever he saw it out of the corner of his eye, he also heard the sound of it moving closer to him.

"I didn't sleep well last night," he said. "No wonder I'm imagining things."

But he was starting to think it wasn't in his imagination.

At one point, he sat down on an old log to wait for the thing to show up again. After a few minutes, it did. From the corner of his eye, he spotted a figure looking at him from behind a tree. It was still for a moment. So was the hunter. He was waiting for it to move before he would look straight at it.

Eventually, he heard the sound of its footsteps, and saw it creep out from behind the tree.

He turned as quickly as he could to see it, but again, it was gone.

"Come out!" he shouted. "Show yourself!"

He then saw it out of the corner of his eye, coming from another direction. When he spun around to look at it, it had vanished. Then he saw it from the other direction. Every time he tried to look right at it, it disappeared from sight. But he could tell it was getting closer.

Then, from the corner of his eye, he saw that it was standing beside a tree only a few feet from him.

The hunter ran over to the tree. The thing was gone.

It was then that he felt a claw dig into his back. He let out a scream of pain and fell to the ground. The claw started dragging him along the ground.

The hunter tried to roll around and see what kind of animal the claw belonged to, but he couldn't. All he could see was the ground in front of him.

They got deeper in the forest, and the hunter started noticing bones all along the ground. Human bones.

Then, the forest went away. He was being brought deep into a dark cave. He screamed for help, but no one could hear him.

Right before it ate him, the hunter saw the thing from the corner of his eye one last time.

THE STATUE

No one liked the new statue in the graveyard. It marked the spot where a famous general was buried. In the day, it wasn't too scary, but at night, it was very frightening.

The statue was of a shrouded woman sitting against the grave. At night, it looked like she was almost alive. Some people said her eyes glowed red, and if you looked at them, you'd go blind. Others told stories about the other dead people in the graveyard rising up to gather around her when midnight fell.

Most people didn't take those stories seriously. The statue was scary, but it couldn't be alive. It also couldn't bring back the dead. Those things just weren't possible.

Still, most people did stay away from it at night. Most people, except for two young men who had just started attending the local college.

They wanted to join a fraternity. Before they could join, they were told they would have to spend one night sleeping next to the statue.

The two young men accepted the challenge. They snuck into the graveyard after dark, before the night watchman arrived.

The night watchman showed up a little bit later. He started walking through the graveyard with his flashlight, making sure there were no trespassers. Suddenly, he heard a terrible scream. It was coming from the direction of the new statue.

The night watchman rushed over. In the distance, it almost looked like two red lights, like eyes, were shining from the statue.

When he got there, they were gone. At first, he couldn't find anything. Then he saw one of the young men. He was lying on the ground. He didn't look hurt, but the night watchman couldn't wake him up. He called for an ambulance.

When the doctors arrived, they said he might never wake up. But he finally did, a few weeks later. The police asked him what happened to the other young man.

He couldn't answer. He couldn't say anything. Sometimes, he would scream for minutes on end, but he never spoke another full word again. He spent the rest of his life in a hospital for crazy people. And they never did find the other young man.

The woods near the mountain were supposed to be a dangerous place. But some people didn't care. They didn't believe the stories about ghosts and monsters and murderers.

One day, a man, woman, and their three children went for a hike there. They didn't return. It was very sad, but many people weren't surprised. They knew you shouldn't go in those woods if you wanted to get home safe.

After a few days, though, the woman stumbled back into town. She had blood all over her clothes. It looked like she hadn't eaten in days.

She told the police a band of crazy men had killed her husband and children. She managed to escape.

Everyone in town tried to take care of her. She was finally able to move back into her old home. But she was never the same. Before her husband and children were killed, she had been a very kind person. Now she was always angry.

She also started reading strange books, and meeting with strange people. In the middle of the night, neighbors would hear them chanting from her home.

One day, she simply disappeared. Everyone assumed she had finally gone crazy. Losing her family had been too great a shock for her.

Over the years, people stopped listening to the old stories about the woods. They'd head up there for hikes and camping. But many of them came back speaking about a woman in white who would float through the trees. If anyone tried to speak with her, she would vanish.

Anyone who saw her would refuse to go back in those woods again. Many of them went crazy not long after seeing her. They would kill themselves weeks, months, sometimes years later.

Some people said it was the old woman. She'd become a witch, and if you saw her, she put a curse on your mind. Sometimes you wouldn't notice anything for a long time. Sometimes you'd go crazy the moment you spotted her.

But if you did see her, you were never truly safe again. You might have escaped the woods, but you would never escape the curse.

LIGHT

Brendan was walking through the forest one night. He liked to play out there sometimes. His parents had told him to get home by dark, but he had lost track of time.

It was hard to see at night. Brendan knew the forest pretty well, but he had never been out there when it was so dark.

Eventually, he spotted a light off in the distance. At first he thought it was from a house. He walked towards it, figuring he must be close to home.

But when he walked towards it, Brendan noticed that the light seemed to move away.

"Maybe it's someone with a flashlight," Brendan told himself. He called out to the person, but he didn't get an answer.

Something about the light made him want to follow it. He felt like it would lead him to safety. He wasn't sure why he felt that way, though. It was like the light was pulling him towards it.

Brendan didn't even notice that the light was actually leading him deeper and deeper into the woods. It was so dark, he didn't know he was actually walking away from home.

The light kept moving deep into the woods, and he kept following it. When it started to move faster, he chased it faster.

Finally, it went so fast that it disappeared from sight.

Brendan was alone. The sounds of the woods surrounded him. Owls hooting. The wind rustling through the trees.

He called out for help, but no one answered.

"I'll be fine," Brendan said. "I can find my way out of here."

But he couldn't. No matter which way he went, it seemed like he was just going deeper into the woods. He tried yelling at the top of his lungs, but it didn't do any good.

When he didn't come home, his parents called the police. For days, they searched the woods. No one ever found him. Some people who lived nearby said that he wasn't really gone, though. Some nights, if you went out into the woods, you might see a strange light off in the distance, and you might, for a moment, hear the cries of a lost little boy.

THE CLOSET

Teddy hated his bedroom closet. It was always dark, no matter what time of day it was. He was sure a monster lived there. But his parents told him it was all in his head. They never believed him when he talked about the monster.

His brother, Bobby, was even worse. Bobby was too old to believe in those types of things. He made fun of Teddy about it all the time.

"One day," Bobby would say, "I'm going to lock you in that closet. Then the monster will get you."

Their parents told Bobby not to say those types of things, but he wouldn't stop. Even when he got in trouble for it, he still kept teasing his little brother.

One night, Bobby decided he would do more than just tease Teddy. Their parents had gone out to dinner. They told Bobby to take care of his little brother until they got back.

But he didn't. They were playing card games in the living room, when Bobby pointed to the corner. "What's that over there?" he said.

As soon as Teddy looked away, Bobby grabbed him from behind and started dragging him to the bedroom closet.

"I'm going to lock you in there for real this time!" he said.

Teddy tried to get away, but Bobby was too strong. He cried and begged his older brother not to lock him in the closet, but Bobby just laughed.

They got to the bedroom. Bobby stuffed Teddy into the closet and held the door closed tight.

Teddy was screaming. Bobby could feel him trying to open the door, but he wasn't nearly strong enough.

Then, after less than a minute, Teddy went silent. He stopped trying to open the door too.

Bobby opened up the closet to see what happened.

Teddy wasn't in there. It was a small space, and there was nowhere to hide.

Bobby looked all over the house. He called out Teddy's name for over an hour. But no one ever saw him again.

ANOTHER CHILD

Mrs. Leeds was very poor. She lived out in the woods with her husband and twelve children. It was very hard taking care of such a large family.

One day, Mrs. Leeds found out she was pregnant with her thirteenth child. She didn't know how she would ever be able to care for another. "Let this child be the devil!" she cried when she learned she was pregnant.

Months passed, until the night came for her to give birth. There weren't many hospitals back in those days, so she had the baby at home. The family gathered around as a nurse helped.

It didn't take long for the baby arrive. For a moment, it looked like a normal child.

Then it started to change. Wings began to sprout from its back. They looked like bat's wings.

Next, it grew a long tail. The child's body started to grow, until it was almost the size of a man. Its feet turned into hooves. Small horns sprouted from its head, and its face turned from a human face into a goat's face.

The monster flew around the room. It killed the nurse, then flew off into the night.

Everyone thought Mrs. Leeds had killed the nurse and her baby when she told the story. No one could prove it, but they knew she hadn't wanted another child. Even though Mr. Leeds and all the other children told the same story, most people just thought they were too scared of Mrs. Leeds to tell the truth.

Because they couldn't prove anything, the police never tried to punish Mrs. Leeds for her crimes.

But soon, strange things started happening. Farmers found many of their animals dead. It looked like they'd been attacked by a gigantic animal. Hunters heard terrible screams in the woods. They almost sounded human, but not quite.

Mrs. Leeds died soon after. Her story lived on, though. Some people even said they saw the monster from time to time. And some people still say they can hear its screams out there in the woods.

OUR DANGEROUS WORLD

These stories didn't happen, but that doesn't mean they couldn't...

BUNNY MAN

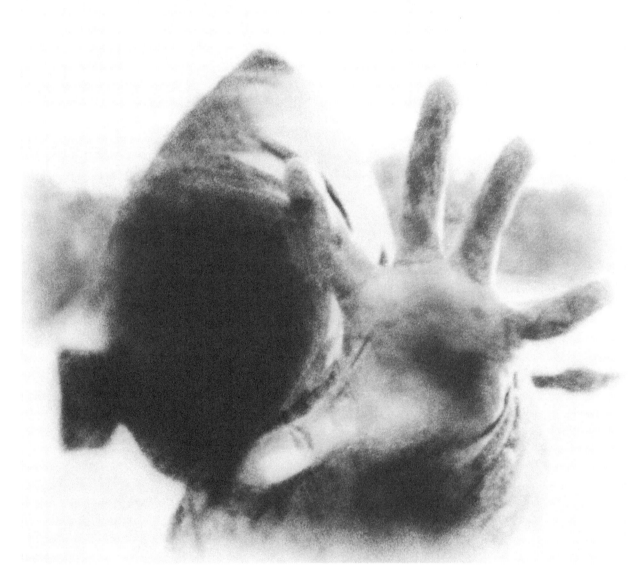

There used to be a hospital for crazy people out by the woods. But more people started building houses in the area. They didn't like the idea of living near insane folks. So they all got together and forced the people who ran the hospital to shut it down.

They couldn't just let the patients free, so they sent them to other hospitals instead. During one of the trips, the bus transporting the patients crashed. The driver died, as well as some of the patients. But a few got away.

The police were able to find most of them within a few days. There was just one patient they could never find. He was a crazy man who had killed many people in the past. The police searched and searched, but there was no trace of him.

Until the bunnies started showing up. People who lived in the area kept finding dead bunnies hanging from trees. They looked half-eaten. Many assumed the patient was hiding out in the woods and eating bunnies to stay alive.

There was a bridge tunnel nearby. People who drove down it sometimes spotted a crazy-looking man hiding in it. They said he carried a hatchet. They would call the police to come look, but by the time they showed up, he was gone.

This went on for years. Then, one night, two local teenagers parked their car near the bridge. They'd heard all the stories, but they didn't believe them. They thought it would be fun to scare themselves, though.

They didn't see anything for a few minutes. Then, suddenly, the back windshield shattered.

The couple turned around. There was a man standing behind the car, but it was too dark to see him clearly.

"You're trespassing," the man said. "Get away!"

They did as they were told, driving off in a big hurry.

When they got home, they found a small hatchet in the backseat.

Again, the police went out in search of the man, but they couldn't find anything. All they found was a message in the tunnel bridge. It was written in blood.

"You'll never catch me."

And they never did.

Richie lived in the city. But that summer, he went to camp in the country. He loved it. There was fishing, and hiking, and swimming. Some nights, before going to sleep, all the campers would tell scary stories.

There were a lot of stories about ghosts, and werewolves, and vampires. But the scariest story was about a killer who escaped from the nearby prison years ago. They said he hid out in the woods around the camp. No one ever caught him, but most were sure he stilled lived out there.

Sometimes, on dark summer nights, he would find lost campers and chop them to pieces with an axe.

Richie pretended the story didn't scare him. But it was hard to sleep after hearing it.

One night, all the campers played hide-and-seek. Richie found a spot under one of the beds and hid there.

A few minutes went by. Then a few minutes more. By the time half an hour had passed, Richie started to get scared. The game should have been over by then.

He crawled out from under the bed and started looking around the camp. No one was in sight. Richie called out the names of the other campers, but no one responded.

He searched for a very long time. He tried to tell himself all the other boys were playing a joke on him. He was the new camper that year. They were just trying to scare him.

He wanted to believe that, but he wasn't so sure.

After almost an hour of searching, Richie headed back to his room. He didn't know where else to go. He hoped if he waited long enough, the other campers would finally show up.

When Richie got to his room, it was dark. He tried to turn on the light, but it wouldn't work.

Richie shone his flashlight through the room. When he pointed it at the back wall, he screamed in terror.

One of the other campers was lying against the wall. There was a dark blood stain on his shirt.

Richie turned around to run, but there was a tall dark figure standing in the doorway, blocking his way. The man was holding a very big axe.

"I found you," he said.

KNOCK KNOCK

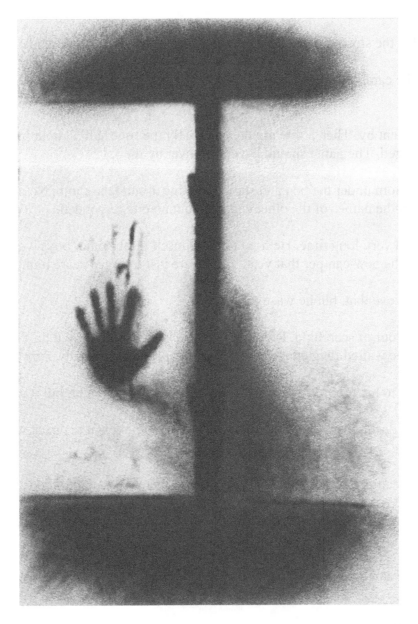

Jimmy and Lisa were brother and sister. One night, their parents went out for dinner. They told them both not to answer the door if they heard anyone knocking. Jimmy and Lisa said they wouldn't.

They watched TV for a few hours. Then there was a knock at the door. They did as their parents told them and ignored it. But the knocking didn't stop. Lisa finally went to see who it was.

A few minutes passed. She didn't come back. Jimmy called out to her, but she didn't respond.

He searched around the house and the yard. She was nowhere to be found.

Jimmy got scared. He ran to a neighbor's house and asked them for help. The neighbor came with Jimmy back to his house.

They looked around, and still couldn't find Lisa. Then the neighbor checked the basement. When she got down there, she screamed.

Lisa was dead on the floor. She'd been strangled to death.

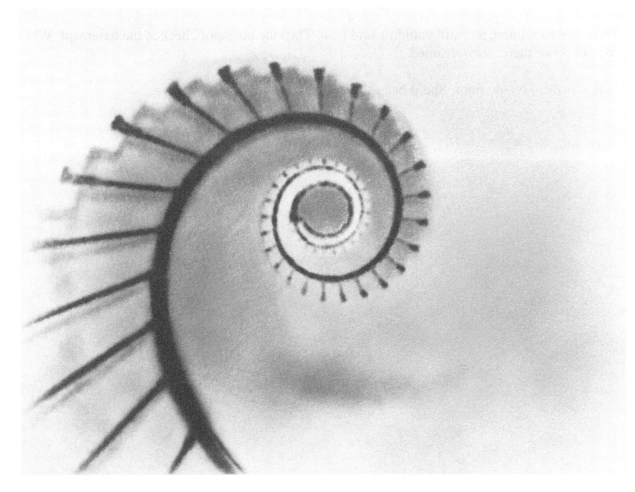

Molly was finally old enough to stay home alone without a babysitter. Her parents were going away for a trip. They wanted to have someone stay with Molly while they were away, but she convinced them not to. She would be fine on her own.

The first night her parents were away, she decided to watch some TV down in the basement. It was a little scary being in the house by herself. She needed something to distract her.

Suddenly, the outside porch light turned on. Molly saw it through the small basement window. It was supposed to only do that when someone was nearby.

Then she heard footsteps upstairs. She called 911 and told them someone broke into the house. The police came by and searched it, but they couldn't find anyone.

The next night, the same thing happened. Molly called the police again. Again, they didn't find anything.

"You know you could get in big trouble for lying to the police," they told her.

Molly said she didn't mean to lie. She really thought someone was in the house.

The third night, Molly was in the basement when she started hearing footsteps coming from upstairs again. She called the police, but they told her they weren't going to come over this time.

Molly didn't know what to do. She stayed down in the basement for a while before hearing someone knock on the door.

Molly was scared, but she went to answer it. Two police officers were there.

"I thought you said you weren't coming," Molly said.

"We weren't going to," one of the officers said. "But when you hung up, we heard another click, like someone hung up on the other line."

They told Molly to wait outside while they searched the house. This time, they went over every inch of the place.

They found a man hiding in the attic. He had some food up there, and two other things: a rope and a knife.

THE CLOWN

It was Becca's first time babysitting for her neighbors, the Johnsons. The night started out easy. The two girls she was watching were well-behaved. They went to sleep soon after Becca arrived.

She decided to watch some TV while she waited for her neighbors to get back. The bigger TV was down in the basement, but when Becca looked down there, she saw a large clown statue in the corner of the room. It scared Becca, and she decided to watch TV upstairs instead.

About an hour later, Mr. Johnson called to ask how things were going.

"Everything's fine," Becca said. "I'm just watching TV right now."

"Feel free to use the bigger TV down in the basement if you want," Mr. Johnson said.

"I would, but that big clown statue you have down there is too scary for me."

Mr. Johnson was silent for a moment. Finally, he said, "We don't have a clown statue. Get the girls out of the house and call the police."

Becca did as she was told. When the police got there, they found an insane man dressed as a clown in the basement. He'd recently escaped from the nearby prison. He'd been sent there for killing a babysitter.

IN THE SNOW

A young couple and their infant daughter moved to a new home near the woods. Soon, their daughter started talking about a man who visited her at night.

The couple assumed their daughter was just making up stories. That all changed one morning.

It had snowed overnight. The man went into the backyard to get a shovel from the shed. That's when he noticed something strange.

There was a set of footprints in the snow. They were big, like a man's. The footprints came from the woods. They led right up to his daughter's bedroom window.

TRULY TERRIFYING

All of these tales are inspired by true accounts.

One night some boys were playing in the yard when they saw a light from the sky land in the woods. They ran inside to grab flashlights, then headed into the woods to find out what the light was.

It was very dark in the forest. Every time an owl or bat flew over them, they jumped in shock. They were afraid they might get lost, but they still wanted to keep going and see what they could find.

The boys were almost ready to turn back when one of them spotted two lights off in the distance. They looked like owl eyes, but they were too big. "Look!" the boy shouted.

All the boys pointed their flashlights in the direction he was pointing.

At first, they couldn't make sense of what they saw. It was too tall to be a person. It was almost twice the size of a grown adult. The thing didn't seem to have feet. It looked like it was almost floating above the ground. It had a big dark hood over its head, and its arms were very thin.

The boys stood in shock for a moment. They were frozen with fear. Finally, one of them started running in the other direction. All the others followed. They ran faster than they ever had before. By the time they got out of the woods, some of them were in tears.

The boys tried to tell their parents what they had seen, but they didn't believe them at first. Their parents thought they had just made the whole story up. But the boys promised they weren't lying. They made their parents call the police.

The police went to the spot where the boys had seen the thing. They didn't find much at first. They almost left, when one of the police officers found something on the ground.

Not far from where the boys saw the thing, there was a clearing in the woods. There were three circles imprinted in the ground. The grass in the circles was all burnt up. It was almost liked something from the sky had landed there.

A NIGHT DRIVE

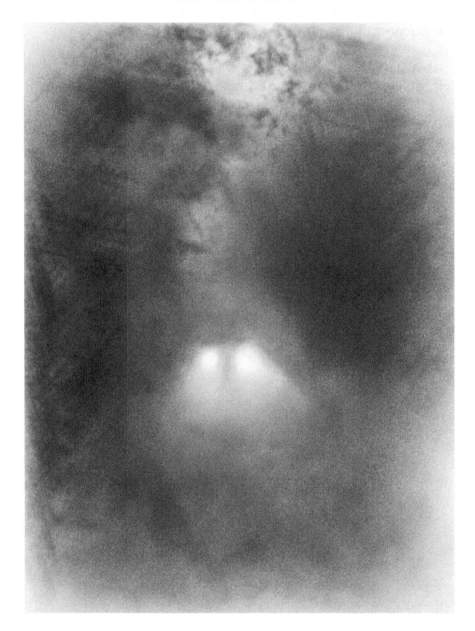

Jenna and Mike had just moved out to the country. They spent a lot of nights driving all around. It was a lot of fun to explore their new home.

One night, they were on a dark, deserted road, when Jenna spotted something in the sky. "What are those?" she said.

"What?" Mike asked.

"Those two lights." Jenna pointed up to a spot right above the car.

Mike looked up. Like Jenna said, there were two small lights flying above them. They seemed to be matching the speed of the car.

"Think it's a plane?" Mike asked.

"I don't think so."

"What else could they be?"

"Mike," Jenna said, "those don't look like airplane lights. Those look like eyes."

Mike looked at them again. They were so high up, it was hard to get a good look, especially while driving. But soon, Mike realized Jenna was right. The two lights looked like animal eyes.

In fact, it looked like they belonged to a very big bird up in the sky. At first Jenna and Mike didn't notice that about them. It was very dark, and they couldn't see much. But now they were both sure it was some kind of animal following them.

"I'll speed up," Mike said. "Let's just get away from them." Something about those eyes scared him.

He drove faster, but the animal just flew faster. Jenna watched it follow them.

"It's coming closer!" she said.

And it was. The thing was flying down towards the car. Now that it wasn't so high up, Mike and Jenna could see it much more clearly.

"What is that thing?" Mike said.

It was still too dark to see it clearly, but it had the shape of a gigantic bat. It was at least as big as a human.

"Drive faster!" Jenna said.

Mike sped up. It was a dark night, and it wasn't safe to drive that fast, but they both wanted to get as far away as they could.

It didn't work. No matter how fast Mike drove, the animal kept up with them. It seemed to be staring at them with its terrible red eyes.

Mike was driving as fast as he could. Still, he couldn't seem to get away from it.

The thing was very close now. It definitely wasn't any sort of bird either of them had ever seen. It had huge wings that never flapped. It also looked like it had arms and legs, like a human, but it was too dark to be sure.

Mike was sure it would catch them. He knew he couldn't drive any faster. But then they saw streetlights up ahead. They were getting close to the nearby town.

Soon, the thing started flying up towards the sky again. By the time Mike and Jenna reached the town, its eyes were only two small dots in the sky. They flew higher and higher until they vanished from sight.

THE COFFIN

Robert Burton owned a farm outside of town with his wife, Margaret. He was a healthy man most of the time.

But one day he got sick. At first he thought it was a cold, but it kept getting worse. One morning, he wouldn't wake up.

Margaret got the town doctor over. He looked Robert over and told Margaret the sad news: Robert had died.

Margaret had been very in love with her husband. No one was surprised when she broke down crying at his funeral.

The night after Robert was buried, Margaret had a dream. Robert was in it. He told her he was still alive, and needed her help.

Most of the time, Margaret didn't believe dreams meant anything. But she was sure this one was different. She went to the doctor and begged him to check the coffin.

The doctor tried to tell Margaret that Robert was certainly dead. He said it was normal to have those types of dreams after losing a loved one.

Margaret didn't care. She insisted they dig up the coffin. She said she would pay whatever it cost.

The doctor gave in. The Burtons were close friends. He thought it would help Margaret get over her loss if she could see her husband was dead.

He got in touch with some folks at the cemetery and had them dig up Robert's coffin. Margaret joined in. She dug faster than anyone, like she knew her husband was running out of time.

When they opened the coffin, Margaret began to cry once again. Robert was dead.

But one of the others diggers noticed something strange. The tips of Robert's fingers were bloody, and there were deep scratch marks on the lid of the coffin.

It almost looked like Robert woke up and had tried to claw his way out.

FACES

Maria was feeding her newborn baby in the kitchen one night. Suddenly, the baby looked down towards the floor and started crying.

Maria looked down to see what had upset her.

To her horror, Maria saw the image of a human face had appeared on the floor. It almost looked like a child's painting. There wasn't a lot of detail, but it looked like the face was of someone who was in pain.

Maria's son destroyed the face and poured new concrete over the spot on the floor.

But the face appeared again the next night. This time there were more. They all looked like they were in pain, or like they were angry.

Maria and her son tried painting over them, but they would keep coming back. Every night, it seemed like there were more of them.

It got so bad that Maria asked her priest to come and bless the house. When he arrived, he told her he knew why the faces kept appearing.

"Why?" Maria asked.

"This land used to be a hospital," he said. "A lot of people died here."

The priest did a ritual to put the spirits at rest. After that, the faces stopped showing up. Over the years, some people stopped believing in the story. They thought Maria had made it all up for attention.

But, even though many tried, they were never able to explain where the faces came from.

CLAW MARKS

Christopher was driving home from work late one night. His parents always let him use their car if he was going to work.

It was very dark out. Christopher heard a thud-thud-thud noise. He realized one of his tires had gone flat.

Christopher pulled over to the side of the road to change the tire. The woods surrounded him on both sides. He wanted to get the job done quickly. He didn't like being out there so late at night.

He'd just finished putting on the new tire when he heard another thud-thud-thud noise, but this one was much louder.

Christopher sprung up to see something terrible running towards him. It was hard to get a good look at it in the dark. It ran on two feet like a person, but it was much bigger than a man, and its skin was green. It almost looked like a cross between a human and a lizard.

Christopher jumped into the car and tried to drive off. Before he could, the monster hopped on the roof of the car and started banging on it. Christopher drove fast, and eventually the thing fell off. He didn't stop to get a good look at it.

When he got home, his parents were angry he was out so late. They were even more angry when they saw the car. The windows were cracked, one of the side mirrors was gone, and there were huge dents all over it.

Christopher told them the story. At first, they didn't believe him. They thought he made the story up to explain why the car was in such bad shape.

But then they took a closer look at the top of the car.

The roof was covered in deep scratches. It almost looked like some sort of huge animal had tried to claw its way in.

HANDS

Not a lot of people liked to drive down the old road through the woods. The road should have been safe, but lots of people still got into accidents when they took it.

Alan didn't know those stories. He was in the area one night visiting some old friends. On his way back home, he decided to take the road. It was a nice night, and he liked driving through the woods on nice nights.

The road was empty except for his car. He drove carefully in case any animals darted out from the woods.

Alan had driven less than a mile, when his car jerked suddenly to the right. He almost went off the road, but he was able to get the steering wheel straight again.

When he looked down at the steering wheel, he nearly froze in terror.

A pair of ghostly hands was gripping it. Without warning, they turned the wheel to the left. Again, Alan was barely able to get the wheel straight again.

He tried to stop the car, but instead, it kept speeding up. He was flying down the road, going much too fast.

The hands once again forced the car to the right. The wheels went off the road, but Alan got control of it again before driving straight into a ditch.

For miles, it went on like this. The ghostly hands kept trying to send the car flying off the road. It took all Alan's effort to keep the car straight. All this time, he was speeding like a madman. He didn't mean to, but it seemed like the car had a life of its own. He was sure he would crash eventually.

Finally, Alan saw he was getting close to the end of the road. For some reason, he knew if he got there he would be safe.

But the hands were stronger than ever. His car would swerve to the right, then suddenly swerve over to the left. There was nothing he could do to stop it.

Alan used all his strength to grip the steering wheel and keep it straight. He was so close to the end of the road, but he wasn't sure how much longer he could hold on.

Finally, he reached the stoplight that marked the road's endpoint. As soon as he got there, the car stopped, and the ghostly hands vanished from sight.

THE UNSOLVED MURDER

Something strange was happening at the Gruber farm. One morning, Mr. Gruber found a set of footprints in the snow. They came from the nearby woods and stopped at the farm. He looked around, but couldn't find the person the footprints belonged to.

Then the noises started. The family heard footsteps coming from some of the other rooms, even when they were sure no one was in them. The family maid quit. She said the house was haunted. Mr. Gruber also noticed that some items would go missing around the farm, like food.

One morning, the Gruber children didn't arrive at school. For a few days, no one saw any member of the family in town.

Some villagers finally headed over to the farm to see what the trouble was.

They found a terrible scene. Every member of the Gruber family was in the barn. So was the new maid. They'd all been killed with an axe.

That's when people remembered all the strange stories Mr. Gruber had told. They didn't think much of them at the time, but now they seemed much more serious. The police figured the killer must have been hiding out in different parts of the farm for a long time. One night, he came out from hiding and killed the Grubers and their maid.

Sadly, they never found the killer.

SCARY SONGS TO SING IF YOU DARE

Traditional folk songs often feature creepy lyrics. These songs are no exception.

IN THE PINES

My girl, my girl, don't lie to me
Tell me where did you sleep last night
In the pines, in the pines
Where the sun don't ever shine
I would shiver the whole night through

My girl, my girl, where will you go
I'm going where the cold wind blows
In the pines, in the pines
Where the sun don't ever shine
I would shiver the whole night through

My girl, my girl, don't lie to me
Tell me where did you sleep last night
In the pines, in the pines
Where the sun don't ever shine
I would shiver the whole night through

My husband, was a hard-working man
Killed a mile and a half from here
His head was found in a driving wheel
And his body hasn't ever been found

My girl, my girl, don't you lie to me
Tell me where did you sleep last night
In the pines, in the pines
Where the sun don't ever shine
I would shiver the whole night through

PRETTY POLLY

Polly, pretty Polly, come go along with me
Polly, pretty Polly, come go along with me
Before we get married some pleasure to see

She got up behind him and away they did ride
She got up behind him and away they did ride
Over the hills and the valleys so wide

They rode a little further and what did they spy
They rode a little further and what did they spy
But a new-dug grave with a spade lying by

Oh Willy, oh Willy, I'm scared of your ways
Oh Willy, oh Willy, I'm scared of your ways
Scared you might lead my poor body astray

Polly, pretty Polly, you've guessed just about right
Polly, pretty Polly, you've guessed just about right
I've dug on your grave the best part of last night

And he stabbed her in the heart and the heart-blood did flow
And he stabbed her in the heart and the heart-blood did flow
Into her grave pretty Polly did go

He threw a little dirt over her and started for home
He threw a little dirt over her and started for home
Leaving nothing behind but the wild birds to moan

And it's debt to the devil, and Willy must pay
And it's debt to the devil, and Willy must pay
For killing pretty Polly and running away

THE UNQUIET GRAVE

Cold blows the wind to my true love,
And gently falls the rain.
I never had but one true love,
And in greenwood he lies slain.

I'll do as much for my true love
As any a young girl may.
I'll sit and mourn all on his grave
For twelve months and a day.

And when twelve months and a day had passed,
The ghost did rise and speak,
"Why do you sit all on my grave
And will not let me sleep?"

'Tis I, 'tis I, thine own true love
That sits all on your grave
I ask one kiss from your sweet lips
And that is all that I crave.

My breast is cold as the clay;
My breath is earthly strong.
And if you kiss my cold, clay lips,
Your days will not be long.

OH, DEATH

Oh, Death
Oh, Death
Won't you spare me over 'til another year?

Well what is this that I can't see
With ice cold hands taking hold of me
Well I am Death none can excel
I'll open the door to Heaven or Hell

Oh, Death someone would pray
Could you wait to call me another day
The children prayed the preacher preached
Time and mercy is out of your reach

I'll fix your feet so you can't walk
I'll lock your jaw so you can't talk
I'll close your eyes so you can't see
This very hour come and go with me

Death I come to take the soul
Leave the body and leave it cold
To drop the flesh up off the frame
Dirt and worm both have a claim

Oh, Death
Oh, Death
Please spare me over 'til another year

My mother came to my bed
Placed a cold towel upon my head
My head is warm my feet are cold
Death is moving upon my soul

Oh, Death how you treating me
You closed my eyes so I can't see
Well you hurting my body you make cold
You run my life right out of my soul

Oh, Death please consider my age
Please don't take me at this stage
My wealth is all at your command
If you will move your icy hands

Oh, the young, the rich, or poor

Are all alike with me, you know
No wealth no land no silver or gold
Nothing satisfies me but your soul

Oh, Death
Oh, Death
Won't you spare me over 'til another year?

BIBLIOGRAPHY

BroDudemars. "What's your favorite urban myth?" *Reddit*. Reddit Inc., 23 Jul. 2013. Web. 5 Oct. 2017.

Capps, Chris. "The 20 Year Gunshot." *Unexplainable.net*. Unexplainable Enterprises LLC, 19 Jun. 2010. Web. 10 Oct. 2017.

Cox, Brent. "The Fantastic Outer Space Tale Of The Flatwoods Monster." *The Awl*. The Awl, 26 Oct. 2012. Web. 25 Sep. 2017.

Lepper, John. "Mothman." *Urban Legends Online*. UrbanLegendsOnline.com, 8 Aug. 2012. Web. 10 Nov. 2017.

Jones, Louis C. *Things That Go Bump in the Night*. Syracuse University Press, 1983.

McCloy, James F. and Ray Miller, Jr. *The Jersey Devil*. Middle Atlantic Press, 1976.

Mikkelson, Barbara. "Home Intruder Poses as Clown Statue." *Snopes*. Snopes.com, 20 Jun. 2014. Web. 10 Nov. 2017.

Moran, Mark and Mark Sceurman. *Weird N.J.* Sterling Publishing Co., Inc., 2005.

Reins, Keith. "The Unquiet Grave." *Folk Songs You Never Sand In Grade School*. Keith Reins, 2017. Web. 13 Oct. 2017.

Schwarz, Rob. "Beyond Belief: The Kid in the Closet." *Stranger Dimensions*. Stranger Dimensions, 28 Mar. 2016. Web. 27 Oct. 2017.

Sprague, Ryan. "Can We Come In? The Lore of the Black Eyed Children." *JimHarold.com*. Jim Harold Media LLC, 27 Oct. 2015. Web. 15 Oct. 2017.

Taylor, Troy. "The Legend of Black Aggie." *Prairie Ghosts*. Troy Taylor, 2000. Web. 31 Oct. 2017.

"The Terrifying Mysteries of the Elfin Forest." *BACKPACKERVERSE*. Backpackerverse. Web. 15 Oct. 2017.

Travelversed Editors. "17 Scariest American Urban Legends." *Travelversed*. QOOL, 21 Oct. 2016. Web. 10 Oct. 2017.

Tucker, Libby. "Cropsey at Camp." VOICES: The Journal of New York Folklore, vol. 32, no. Fall-Winter 2006. Web. 10 Oct. 2017.

"Urban legend Black Annis makes the trip from England to the Midwest." *A Gothic Curiosity Cabinet*. Gothic Horror Stories, 2017. Web. 12 Oct. 2017.

Wikipedia contributors. "Bélmez Faces." Wikipedia, The Free Encyclopedia. Wikipedia, The Free Encyclopedia, 13 Oct. 2017. Web. 4 Dec. 2017.

Wikipedia contributors. "Bunny Man." Wikipedia, The Free Encyclopedia. Wikipedia, The Free Encyclopedia, 3 Dec. 2017. Web. 4 Dec. 2017.

Wikipedia contributors. "Hairy Hands." Wikipedia, The Free Encyclopedia. Wikipedia, The Free Encyclopedia, 28 Oct. 2017. Web. 29 Nov. 2017.

Wikipedia contributors. "Hidebehind." Wikipedia, The Free Encyclopedia. Wikipedia, The Free Encyclopedia, 2 Aug. 2017. Web. 4 Dec. 2017.

Wikipedia contributors. "Hinterkaifeck murders." Wikipedia, The Free Encyclopedia. Wikipedia, The Free Encyclopedia, 20 Nov. 2017. Web. 29 Nov. 2017.

Wikipedia contributors. "In the Pines." Wikipedia, The Free Encyclopedia. Wikipedia, The Free Encyclopedia, 1 Nov. 2017. Web. 29 Nov. 2017.

Wikipedia contributors. "Lizard Man of Scape Ore Swamp." Wikipedia, The Free Encyclopedia. Wikipedia, The Free Encyclopedia, 30 Aug. 2017. Web. 4 Dec. 2017.

Wikipedia contributors. "O Death." Wikipedia, The Free Encyclopedia. Wikipedia, The Free Encyclopedia, 20 Nov. 2017. Web. 4 Dec. 2017.

Wikipedia contributors. "Premature burial." Wikipedia, The Free Encyclopedia. Wikipedia, The Free Encyclopedia, 8 Sep. 2017. Web. 4 Dec. 2017.

Wikipedia contributors. "Pretty Polly (ballad)." Wikipedia, The Free Encyclopedia. Wikipedia, The Free Encyclopedia, 14 Oct. 2017. Web. 4 Dec. 2017.

Wikipedia contributors. "Will-o'-the-wisp." Wikipedia, The Free Encyclopedia. Wikipedia, The Free Encyclopedia, 3 Dec. 2017. Web. 4 Dec. 2017.

NOTES

ON THE HUNT

Scary Stories to Tell in the Dark introduced me to *Things That Go Bump in the Night*, the classic collection of New York folklore from Louis C. Jones. Luckily, my childhood library had a copy. It's an ideal book to read if you love this genre, and is the source of this tale.

THE BULLET

Although this story is often passed off as true on the internet, research indicates it's actually a myth. For readers interested in learning more, research the Henry Ziegland case.

CAMPING

This story is based on an account reported in *Weird N.J.* It supposedly took place on Clinton Road in West Milford. I grew up hearing these stories, and included another Clinton Road tale in the previous book in this series.

BLACK EYES

The legend of the Black-Eyed Children first gained traction in the mid 1990s. Although many people claim to have had actual encounters with these beings, they've entered the realm of myth.

ANNIE'S HOUSE

Despite being one of the most well-known scary stories from folklore, the tale of Black Annis remained unknown to me until I began researching this book. It was too iconic to not include.

HIDDEN

The Hidebehind is a mythical creature from American legend. It's said to change its size so that it's small enough to hide behind a tree or other object whenever someone tries to look at it. In early settler days, the Hidebehind was often blamed if loggers didn't return to camp after venturing into the woods.

THE STATUE

The legend of Black Aggie is another classic legend of American folklore I remained unfamiliar with until I began researching this book. This retelling is based on several accounts.

THE WITCH OF THE WOODS

Again, scary stories give you the opportunity to learn about other cultures and places, even within your own country. This very creepy tale has its roots in California, where legend states that Elfin Forest is haunted.

LIGHT

The will-o-the-wisp, known by many other names in many other parts of the world, is so ubiquitous in world folklore that many believe it to be real. This account is based on the general details of the legend, and no one particular account.

THE CLOSET

The television series *Beyond Belief: Fact or Fiction*, dramatized this tale, reporting that it was a true account. However, it was later learned that the young boy in the story escaped from the closet via a ceiling panel, and was found later.

ANOTHER CHILD

The Jersey Devil is one of American folklore's classic characters. This retelling is based on popular legends of its birth. I plan on including other tales about this being in future books.

BUNNY MAN

Although the legend has circulated for decades, the internet has significantly boosted the popularity of the Bunnyman Bridge legend. This account is based on details from several different accounts.

I FOUND YOU

The Cropsey legend is very popular throughout New York State summer camps. This retelling is fairly original, intended to make it more "story-shaped" than it typically is. Cropsey has also served as the inspiration for numerous slasher films, including *Friday the 13th*. The remote camp setting puts it firmly in the American Gothic tradition.

KNOCK KNOCK

Urban legends often speak to adolescent fears. As we grow up and become adults, we realize how vulnerable we can be. Like many other tales, this story warns children about what could happen when their parents begin to play a less protective role.

THE ATTIC

This urban legend bears obvious similarities to classic tales like "The Babysitter." It, too, highlights a fear that is very common in adolescents. The idea of unknowingly sharing a living space with an intruder is a popular trope in many scary stories.

THE CLOWN

This story also belongs in the category of tales like "The Babysitter." It rose in popularity starting around 2004, when versions of it started showing up in email chains.

IN THE SNOW

This short, creepy tale, is inspired by an actual experience a relative of mine had. The detail about the daughter speaking about a man who visits her was added, but otherwise, it's a fairly honest retelling.

SOMETHING IN THE WOODS

Some stories stay with you forever. I must have been a very young child when I first read about The Flatwoods Monster. It's stuck with me ever since.

A NIGHT DRIVE

This tale is a modified version of a story told by two couples, who allegedly encountered the Mothman. As with the Jersey Devil, I plan on sharing more Mothman stories in future books.

THE COFFIN

Before modern medicine made it possible to confirm whether an individual was truly dead before burying them, premature burials did occur. This is a fictionalized story, but people have been buried alive in the past.

FACES

This tale is based on the story of the Belmez Faces, another story that I read as a child and never forgot. Details have been condensed and altered to facilitate this retelling.

CLAW MARKS

The Lizard Man of Scape Ore Swamp may have achieved somewhat mythic status in South Carolina, but many report having actually encountered the being. This story is based on an allegedly true tale.

HANDS

There are several roads throughout the world where drivers have reported seeing a set of hands appear on the steering wheel, taking control of their vehicles. This retelling is a combination of details from several accounts.

THE UNSOLVED MURDER

The Hinterkaifeck murder case is truly chilling. The retelling here is based very closely on the actual facts of the case.

IN THE PINES

This folk song has been performed by everyone from Lead Belly to Nirvana. It's a personal favorite. The lyrics used here are based primarily on one of Lead Belly's recordings.

PRETTY POLLY

This traditional murder ballad has roots in the British Isles, but versions of it are also popular through Appalachia.

THE UNQUIET GRAVE

The supernatural elements of this folk song easily earned it a place in this book. The lyrics printed here are based on a popular version, although as is often the case with folk music, there are many variants.

OH, DEATH

Scary stories represent very basic fears. Such is often the case with folk music, too.

ABOUT THE AUTHOR

Joe Oliveto is a freelance writer who has loved scary stories his entire life. He wrote this book, and its predecessor, to share just a few of the creepy tales he's come across over the years. He currently lives in New York City, and can be reached via email at Joseph.Oliveto@gmail.com.

Be sure to find the *Scary Stories to Tell if You Dare* page on Facebook!

Made in the USA
Las Vegas, NV
13 July 2024

92281167R00039